NEW
INFINITY

METATRON PRESS
WWW.METATRON.PRESS

New Infinity
© 2022 Bára Hladík

Published by Metatron Press
Montréal, Québec

First printing
Printed in Québec, Canada

All rights reserved

Editor | Lauren Turner
Cover art | Chandra Melting Tallow
Author photo | Colene AuCoin

Library and Archives Canada Cataloguing in Publication

Title: New infinity / Bára Hladík.
Names: Hladík, Bára, author.
Description: Poems.
Identifiers: Canadiana (print) 20220190925 | Canadiana (ebook) 20220190941 |
ISBN 9781988355245 (softcover) | ISBN 9781988355320 (PDF)
Classification: LCC PS8615.L33 N49 2022 | DDC C811/.6—dc23

We acknowledge the support of the Canada Council for the Arts.

NEW INFINITY

BÁRA HLADÍK

METATRON PRESS
WWW.METATRON.PRESS

NEW INFINITY

The Face	9
Robo	10
Speed Bump	19
Old Dogs	26
The Ringing	29
Book of Shadows	31
Bed of Dreams	47
My Friend	50
The Touch	52
Book of Mirrors	59
The Note	84
The Park	85
The Same	89
The Date	90
The Break Up	91
Book of Dreams	95
Sound of Your Cry	119
The Walls	122
New Infinity	123

*for those surviving
and those we've lost*

The mind was dreaming.
The world was its dream.

- Jorge Luis Borges

The Face

The face is a portrait of fear, the walls pulse. I am speaking to someone about elliptical time. Out of the window, the light on the leaves becomes another window, opening to a cloud, to the light, to the waking of a deep ache, a deep drone, to a burning sharp breath, to an unforgiving claw torquing a sharp screw, screwing my eyes open to a room, to the light on the leaves out the window, to writhing my spine cracking it open, popping, stumbling to cold water on my pulsing face, burning, moving, stretching, falling, crashing, burning, cracking, pushing, pulsing, burning,

    cracking,

        pushing,

            pulsing.

Robo

When he tried for the first and last time to paint a horse, he executed it perfectly. I was devastated. There was nothing more to be said. He looked at me proudly. This made things worse. I ran to my room and closed the door.

Later in the evening, I knew he could hear me on the phone through the door. *He has no expression.* He hadn't been able to hear through the door in his previous version. I recalled past moments when he had seemed *expressive*. These times now carried a light green hue in my memory, as if the prints had been left in the sun too long.

We met for dinner with friends. She talked about her embroidered wall hangings of landscapes and small dogs. He shook his glass and crunched ice in his teeth.

"So how are the numbers?" he asked. She bumped him under the table and frowned. *Don't*, she breathed, and glanced at me. He leaned his elbows on the table.

"Same as always," said Robert. "There's always more numbers." He lurched his fist in what looked like an attempt at a jovial air-punch but turned out to look more like a hydraulic pump. My friend shifted in her seat.

"I heard you were promoted," she raised her eyebrows.

"Assistant Coordinator of Data," Robert replied.

"Should we look at the menu," I said.

The first signs concerned grocery receipts. He was increasingly interested in reading receipts. Then, instructions for various household items. I would find myself following a strange sound through the apartment just to find him reciting the small print of the laundry detergent under his breath. He had just started a new job and had to work very hard. I assumed it was a memory exercise from his new work. He was always saying that his work mates were like encyclopedias. I began to hide the receipts, the instructions. I began leaving drawings around the house, old photographs, poetry. It was as if they weren't even there. Once, I showed him a photograph I had found of my family. He studied it for a moment, nodded, and handed it back. I read him a poem from a collection given to me by my grandmother. When I finished reading, he looked at me and blinked. I stood and went to the kitchen and returned holding a receipt I had stashed in the flour. He stood abruptly. It was the closest thing to excitement I had seen in weeks.

We watched geese at the park.

"Aren't they wise, those geese? They fly so far every year, then back to Canada," I said as I leaned over the cement railing of the park bridge, smelling the wind as we watched geese pecking at the grass.

"Their average lifespan is 12 years. Their average weight is 23.5 pounds at full size," he recited, his shoulders square, his arms holding the railing at ninety degrees.

"Where would you go," I asked, "if you migrated every year?"

"The majority of humans migrate for economic reasons. I am financially secure," he said.

"Okay, whatever. People migrate for holidays, where would you go, if you could?" I asked again.

He turned to me, and for a minute I thought I saw him again, a flicker in his eye. But he turned back, square with the railing, and said, "The company might send me to Houston. You too, of course."

"What is with this company," I said, throwing my hands from the railing like birds taking flight. "There's no way I'm moving to Houston."

"Not moving," he said. "Collecting data. And visiting, of course."

"You never used to say *of course*," I said.

We met at a dinner party shortly after I landed my first job. You could say it was the right time. He always wore a clean shirt and was prone to anxiety. I was into making lace. He admired this, often comparing typing algorithms on a keyboard to making lace.

"You spend time practicing, like a muscle," he said looking at the geese. "Like how you make lace, it alters your state of mind. You become unconscious in the process, but more efficient." He sat on the grass next to me with his legs crossed in Lotus, something he had started to do in the Beginning Stages, as they called it.

"But I don't," not wanting to accuse, "*upgrade*," I said as I ripped at the short grass in front of me, making several small piles.

"*Change is Improvement*," he said, echoing the company's upgrade slogan as he straightened his spine.

Shifts are natural, but was this? I thought. For some reason, *natural* was the question I was asking. "Natural flavour," I remembered he exclaimed once as he cracked a cold soda. "There's nothing like it." He preferred artificial grapefruit, never sweetened.

"It's programming," I said to the torn grass spiral I had created. "Not the same."

At three minutes to 5 p.m., Robert was making it count. If he stayed on track, he could complete fifteen algorithms before the end of the day. He recalled earlier times when he would sit back and let these final minutes slide by, savouring the anticipation of the beginning of the weekend. Now, it felt like the end of the week. He no longer had the same craving for the weekend; he craved executing numbers. He understood the weekend was necessary for rest, but it came with a certain stagnation. It wasn't quite a feeling.

He sat back, complete. Others in the office were already standing. He had found it odd at first, that the company insisted on upgrading, as they called it, and he had outright refused the first time. But as he got more comfortable in his position, he couldn't help but envy his coworkers who had gone through the process. They were simply more effective.

"Something is wrong," I said when he got back from work. "I'm not ok."

He sat across our apartment and gave me a blank stare. I stared back.

"I'm... something is wrong," I repeated, starting to pace.

He remained still.

"It's my back. I'm in pain, I'm tired. I sleep and sleep and I'm still tired." I paced digging my hand into my lower back as if trying to grab on to the pain and pull it out. He folded his hands.

"Have you been to the doctor?" he said, gathering facts.

"I went two weeks ago, remember? The doc said I should sleep and exercise," I said. "Which I've been doing, but it just feels like my back is filling up with, like, a toxic liquid."

"Toxic liquid," he said.

I stopped in my tracks and turned on my heel, looking him directly in the eyes.

"Does your upgrade mean you don't get metaphors anymore?" I was still digging my hand into my hip. He looked down at his hands.

On Monday, I called in sick. I slept fourteen hours, woke up for two hours to eat and shower and fell asleep for another twelve. I called in sick for the rest of the week. He came home after work every day with groceries, made food, watched TV, then fell asleep whether I was conscious or not. I woke at odd hours to heat up his leftovers, try to get some liquids down, and return to bed. Sometimes I would wake up in the afternoon and see the sun come through the window, but getting myself to the ray of sun was impossible.

"I'm a mess," I said when he got back from work one day. My hair was an elaborate nest of lost buns and knots, dried tears shone under my eyes like the paths of bygone slugs. He sat next to me on the bed, "It's ok, just rest. I will make dinner."

My friend called him at work. "She needs medical attention now," she said. "You can't just leave her to die in that apartment."

"Yes. Yes, of course," he had said as he wrote PD into his calendar for the following week. "I will take a Personal Day."

Robert methodically stacked pills on top of plastic containers. His upgrades were now complete, and he had become very accurate at preparing food and medication. She was in bed as usual as he locked the door behind him to go to work.

On the train, he gazed vacantly at the opposite wall. Stops came and went, people boarded and disembarked. Across from him sat an old woman with white hair and wrinkled skin. She watched him. She looked into his face, right into his eyes. She remained still, but it felt as if she was coming towards him. He heard her voice in his head whisper, *"If you're not here, where are you?"*

He got off the train and walked through the station with the crowd like a fish in water. It was rush hour. The woman's words rippled in his brain, throughout his consciousness. *Where are you.* On my way to work. *Where are you.* At the train station. *On planet*

Earth! He told himself. He felt unstable as if walking on sand. The crowd moved steadily forward around him. His palms felt wet, his gut ached with nausea. His upgrades were supposed to increase stamina and prevent illness and discomfort, but his whole body throbbed in some unexplained reaction.

He got out of the station and caught a cab home. He crawled into bed fully clothed. She was deeply asleep, heavy. She began to stir when he put his arms around her but didn't wake. He felt her warm soft flesh, smelled her deep sleep. He counted twenty-two lashes lining her closed eyelids.

I opened my eyes slowly. He was smiling.

"What is it?" I whispered.

"I'm going to downgrade," he said a little too fast. In two years of going to doctors over and over, I had become used to his detached, calculated demeanour. He took care of scheduling appointments, tracking medications, finances. I had stopped calling him Robert a long time ago. I'd called him Robo a few times, but he didn't laugh. *You're so lucky to have that kind of man*, an administrator had told me. *What kind*, I thought. He continued to get regular upgrades while my health rapidly degraded.

"Downgrade," I repeated with my eyes closed. I let it sink into the ocean of my mind. "I didn't know you could do that."

"I'll find a way," he said. We held each other, breathing slow, knowing there was no way to revert upgrades.

"What about your job?" I asked.

"I'll figure it out."

He left to work the next morning with the same calculated step, as if revived. I woke late, nursing my struggling corpse. Sometimes it would take me hours to manage to eat. I didn't always get dressed or brush my teeth. Most days, I had no appetite, yet I was nauseous from hunger. I needed to move my stiff joints but was paralysed by fatigue. Today my head was pounding from the pressure in my spine. By 2 p.m., I rolled out of bed to the floor and crawled to the shower with my eyes closed. The hot water helped me get standing. I put the kettle on for coffee and sat in the kitchen in a towel, then took my coffee back to bed.

In the afternoon, I laid a blanket on the floor. I rolled from side to side like a pencil. I rolled around loose. I stretched into shapes. I dipped a small paint brush in water and softly painted my legs. I told them to take their time, it didn't matter that I was missing the sun. When the time comes, we would take the open sky however she was.

Speed Bump

I was just among the whales. I hang somewhere in water or mud listening to whales move through water until the snakes weave my muscles. They swim up the center of my spine and fill my lymph with soft poison. They tie knots in my skull and lay eggs in my temples. There is nowhere for them to go, so they push and coil, push and coil. I rise carefully because I'm so full of snakes. They flex and roll and bite as I move to the shower to calm them with hot, hot water.

My roommates are working at the hotel or jackhammering concrete. I am home, a balancer of spoons. I balance a spoon on my windowsill for getting out of bed, a spoon on a pile of laundry for getting dressed. I save ninety spoons for the doctor's appointment. If you balance a spoon everywhere you go and never run out, you don't pass out.

I leave thirty spoons between cans of beans at the store. My roller is a ball and chain of heavy roots. Every step up the street leaves an imprint the size of France. The speed bump is a tragedy, I contemplate death. In another time, women who lived with snakes were burned. Now, they are forgotten. I get tangled between my cane and my roller and leave my body near Salsbury. The season is changing. I sit by a witch hazel. The thin yellow flowers reach to me. A drop of water winks, even though there hasn't been any sun in months.

I wake up on the couch and my spoons and roots are scattered on the floor. I collect the spoons, then the roots. I put them on the shelves. I rest, I breathe. I cook a heap of food between naps, face down on the kitchen table. I move my hips slow to the onions singing in hot oil and Joni's soft voice on tape. She had something like snakes, or was it bugs? I'd rather have a whale. One big slow whale.

On the bus, I glimpse the chicken processing plant. It smells wrong. Up the alley, there is a row of workers in stained yellow rubber aprons marching out one door and in another. Some of them must have snakes they don't talk about. I leave a pile of spoons in the priority seating for someone with piranhas.

The waiting room is in a far-off nether region of the hospital: an old TV on mute, a couple of people wearing fleece, some carpeted chairs, a clock. I take a seat and balance thirteen spoons on the armrest. I frown at the clock because it doesn't tell the time, it tells contrasts. Like, you vs. your birth, you vs. your appointment, you vs. snakes. But the planet spins around the sun in an ellipse and time slips around like light, like when you are waiting for relief and the only thing you can do is count the days you've been alone with your snakes.

"Course I don't give a damn about what I'm wearing," said the woman to her old man. "I'm dying." He was looking at a magazine he picked up from the stacks of last year's *Cosmopolitan*. He flipped twice and put it back. "But shit, so are you," she laughed and patted his thigh.

The clock was moving, we weren't. My leg was sticking straight out beside my cane. The man stood up and marched to the counter.

"Our appointment was an hour and a half ago," he said to the secretary.

She nodded and clicked around on her computer. Her stringy blonde bangs arched above her drawn eyebrows. "Sorry sir, there's nothing we can do."

I laugh. Well, I laugh without laughing. In silence, with no joy. There is nothing you can do in the white-walled chamber that schedules pain. The administrator clicks, the clock ticks. Patient, yes, I am.

The man returns to the woman's side and they lean their heads together. She is dying and her time is spent amongst rubber plants and posters of skeletons.

She could be at home amongst her dahlias. A cockroach slips out her ear and scurries up the wall. We all sit here, contained in our bodies, our thoughts afloat. My thoughts take a vacation to the desert. It's too hot and the sky is so big it burns my lips.

A mother brings a boy into the waiting room. They check in with the administrator and sit down. His legs stick straight off the chair. I picture him in a lounger, eighty-three years old. He looks wide at his mother who hands him a kid's book from the stack next to the magazines. The dying woman asks the boy what his name is. His little hands clutch and rub and pat the thin metal arm of the chair. He looks to his mother for directions. She raises her eyebrows.

"Why cockroaches?" he whispers.

My aunt had an undiagnosed condition. They gave her antidepressants and said her thought patterns were to blame. Years later, they found she had maggots in her thyroid. Maggots who are now addicted to antidepressants.

The administrator calls my name. I shuffle to the counter, lean my cane on the wall. She peers down at me with her vacant blue eyes. "Follow the nurse," she says. The nurse walks three steps ahead of me through doors down a hallway to another waiting room. I drop too many spoons along the way, but she doesn't notice. "The doctor will be with you shortly," she says and leaves. Waiting room 2.0.

Every chair filled except one. People looking at their phones, sleeping on the floor, reading magazines, whispering. Some people looked at the wall, others looked at the floor. An older lady with large thick glasses kept pushing her thin hair out of her face and looking at me. I wondered if she could see my snakes. A couple in their thirties both wearing white collared shirts were doing a crossword. I wasn't in the mood for watching. I wanted to be deep in warm water listening to the sounds of whales. But I'd been waiting for this appointment for nine months.

I couldn't breathe, so I read a diagram of a diaphragm. The diaphragm, it says, *is the musculomembranous partition separating the thoratic and abdominal cavities.* Do the doctors know how to breathe? Do their diaphragms *relax convex, but flatten as it contracts during inhalation?* They fill paperwork for dying people, they glimpse thirty-two devastating lives in eight hours. Do they breathe?

Another nurse gave me paperwork. Name, address, medical history. A document of my phenotypic variations from the average human. I finished quick and sat with my completed document on my lap. I read the document five times. I whispered to the snakes and massaged my hip. I stood and stretched and sat down. I drew triangles above the word PATIENT and circles above INTAKE. People came and went. A young girl with a red shirt, who had come after me, was already with a doctor somewhere. Even the lady with the fanny pack had come and gone. I'd been forgotten.

I wrestled snakes down my back as I went down the hall to the nearest desk. The man told me I was at the wrong desk and I should go to the check-in counter down the hall. The counter down the hall was closed. I made my way back to the original waiting room and checked in for the second time. The woman told me to take a seat.

"I've already been here for hours," I said. "I had an appointment at one."

"You're just going to have to wait," she said without a glance. I clenched my fist on the counter, then laid down my palm. She was probably just as tired as I was. The most successful part of the system is that no one is to blame.

I watched the clock, seconds spun, minutes merged. Every minute more snakes. Mindfulness, they teach you, is great for chronic snakes. So is medical attention.

"Why are you here?" asked the doctor, finally. He looked at me through a fishbowl.

"I have snakes, I'm full of snakes," I said.

"On a scale of one-to-ten, how bad are your snakes?" he asked while a blue fish circled his nose.

"There are ten snakes in my hips, thirteen in my spine, four in my ankles, two in each knuckle on my hands. In the morning, there are thirty-two snakes in my neck and twenty-five in each elbow. I've had snakes for six years, two months, three days," I said sitting neat like my mother taught me, so that professionals would believe what I say.

"Your tests don't show any evidence of snakes," the doctor said through the fishbowl. "Come back in eight months."

When I get home, the mail tells me my income was eight thousand dollars last year and it was all debt, but now I can apply to go to the pool for free. I climb the stairs one step at a time, so I stay aerobic. The snakes are fighting with each other. I tell them to get their shit together, it's just a few more stairs. A snake bites my hip and my eyes fill with water. I breathe in to tell them there's no danger; it's just me, trying to get up steps. In group therapy, they say, *love yourself, forgive yourself.* I love you, I tell my snakes. They swim and coil and burn me under my skin. Thank you, I say to my snakes and I swim with them, at last, to join the whales.

Old Dogs

My dog lies on the floor and so do I. My head on his chest, his paw on my leg. His hair falls out but smells good, like him. I run my hand along his fur and gather a handful of white hair. His white hairs have followed me for years, hung on my pants in middle school, fell off behind me as I ran for the bus. His hairs falling off my family as they ran in and out the door.

I used to run too, so did my dog. His skin so loose as a puppy, ready to be grown into, wobbling as he runs, chasing shadows of butterflies. He grew, we grew. We all ran.

Sometimes he'd fall down the stairs, seizure at the bottom. His eyes roll back, he shakes, foams at the mouth. I put my hand on his chest, protect his head, until he comes back, looks into my eyes, asking what happened.

My dog slows, limps. My dog's hips fuse. I limp, pretending to not limp. I limp, sometimes for too many days. I say it's a bruised tailbone. It goes away until it comes back. It comes back and I stay home until it goes away. I stay home with my dog until it goes away, but it comes back before it goes away. My dog and I, laying on the floor, until it goes away.

People look at my dog and say, *haha wow that dog's got problems*. They look at me and say, *at least you look great!* People look at my dog and say, *poor guy, what a good boy*. They look at me and say, *have you tried yoga? Running?*

My dog gets diagnosed with autoimmune disease five years before I do. The vets believe my dog, prescribe anti-inflammatory medications. The doctors tell me I'm depressed, prescribe me antidepressants. The vets say, it's episodic, degenerative. The docs say, it's mental illness, a lack of motivation.

I visit my family, lay with my dog. My family runs in and out the door. I don't know how to tell them that something is happening to me. Like, not something you can run with. Something like the dog.

I get a new doctor, who prescribes an MRI. The MRI comes in, they say they see it, my joints are fused. It's episodic, degenerative, starts young. Just like my dog.

My dog limps, still chasing butterfly shadows. Smiling, despite the pain. Excited, despite stumbling down the stairs. He loses an eye, still looks at me panting, smiling. He's so old, they say, even though he is young.

It gets harder. The last time I see him I tell him it's ok if he dies. I thank him for laying with me when no one else would. Understanding me when no one else did. Showing me joy exists within pain, reminding me to never stop chasing butterfly shadows. I gather white hair on my palm, spread it on my pants, my sweater, my hair. I bury myself in white hair while we lay together like old dogs, waiting for it to go away.

The Ringing

"I can't stop thinking about degenerating," I said, sitting on the edge of a rocking chair. Before I didn't know, I was just overwhelmed. But now I know. I can't stop imagining it. That's what the pain is. Bones degenerating.

My roommate stirs onions on the stove. "I'll tell you what," he glances at me. "I woke up one morning with a ringing in my ear. It was so loud I couldn't sleep. It didn't stop for weeks. I didn't sleep. I was going crazy. I didn't know what to do. One day all of a sudden, it didn't matter. I stopped listening. It's still ringing right now. I've just accepted that it's there."

Book of Shadows

I wake in the night. The tree outside dances in the dark. I pull a card: Seven of Clubs. I know something is coming. The wind shakes the window and my lungs rattle. The stillness greets movement. In the dark, I reach for the spine of a book. I don't open it but I know what's inside.

Siri, what is a virus?

here's what I found.
a virus is a small infectious agent.
that replicates only inside.
the living cells. of an organism.
a pathogen. or. producer of.
"passion." or. "suffering."

(too small to see. without magnification.)
invades humans. animals. other living hosts.
their growth. and reproduction.
can cause disease.

smell the bed sheets / my mother says / reminds me of when my mother / couldn't / my mother says / it's the smell / of dirty sheets / brings me back to / my mother / always / shaking pills / in her pockets / never cleaning / never / really there / my mother says / cleaning / the sheets / while i sweat / sweat / fever / fever / slices / half an onion / wraps cloth / around my throat / i'm coughing / coughing / she's mixing / mixing / honey with onion / as i sweat / sweat / the sheets / the dirty sheets / like my mother / and my daughter / says my mother / always / back to the sheets / always back / to the sweat

Siri, what is H1N1?

here's what i found.
the 2009. pandemic.
death toll of 284 000 lives.

in quarantine / i survive / weeks of fevers / nurses bring trays / count white blood cells / i dream of doctors / who don't believe me / but it / happened here / i tell them / in this hospital / i've been / sick / ever since

normally the system.
can tell the difference.

between foreign cells.
and your own.

an autoimmune disease.
mistakes your body. as foreign.

releases autoantibodies.
to attack. a foreign invasion.

the body / permeable / reflecting / to the self / encounters / to the cell / how translation / occurs / how emotion / informs / the molecular narratives / that structure / pain / the pupil contracts / to light / a mirror / to the sky / like skin / sensing / surroundings / shaking / shifting / self / the sensation / of being / in a body / the sensation / of being / in a waiting room / being / a being / a benign / being / in a room / waiting / in pain / for the words / for being / in this body / in pain

mirror in my cell
subatomic ghost

thymus of faces
i try to know

why do we fight
our cells, ourselves

my mother's mother's
molecular mimicry

if the cell falls into
itself is it a memory

if the self falls into
itself is it a dream

if i / write my tears / does that make me / tangible / i just / never thought / i'd be / here / wondering / where i am / after all these years / i carry paperwork / i should have done / i know there was / someone / i was supposed to call / tick / tock / two years / goes by / my blankets / change shape / so must i / it takes me / four months / to deposit / a cheque / i'd rather / call a sick girl / to remind her / she exists / drain / drain me down / a drain / if they don't / drain me / i'll drain / in the rain / drain / on the system / drain / in pain

Siri, what is Ankylosing Spondylitis?

on a scale of one to ten / one being no difficulty at all / ten being / the worst pain you've / ever / felt / ten being / difficult to the point / where you say / I can't do this / level of fatigue and exhaustion / to difficulty putting on socks and shoes / to what does a nine *feel* like / to i can't do this / to difficulty getting up from laying on the floor / to what is your energy envelope / to number of hours / of hours / of hours / of stiffness in the morning / to *i can't* / difficulty standing from an armless dining chair / *quite get up* / to eight / to nine / to level of difficulty getting through a regular day / to can you please characterize / *regular day* / one to ten to too much / too little or not enough / what is the percentage of / pain increase during / peak hours

ankylosing spondylitis.
is an inflammatory disease.
that over time. causes the bones.
in your spine. to fuse.

degeneration
is a natural phenomenon
in which you become
aware of death

as you reach
to flowers

falling
from sky

the silence / of hours / when others / are busy / i'm so busy / in my body / i can't move / and yet / i exist / if i exist / and can't move / am i a philosopher / my thinking hangs / floats / fogs / i write / three sentences / an entire winter / what are the philosophical implications / of being / too sensitive / to the world / where does the time go / waiting / to be conscious / it's ok / i have a candle / i light every morning / i have a magnolia / i watch change / she is bare / most of the year / but erupts / in spring thick labias / reaching for the sky / as i thank her / i cry / to cure myself / i cry

what is
     a body

envision / infinity / is it visible / is it palatable / is there / radiographic evidence / this spine / in this civilization / this indivisible divinity / this spondyloarthropathy / these unkind cytokines / can i just be / this body / is invisible / but i'm still in it / and you're still looking / at my light blockers / not seeing my eyes / i envision / this infinity / this / unlucky / lucky / indivisible divinity / is this not intimacy / must i see clearly / to be here / to be free / i don't have / a lack of vision / i have too much light / in my eyes / glare / must mean / i'm alive / trying to be part / of a civilization / i don't know / where i'm going / but i've got radiographic evidence / there's somewhere / i've been

a material form
for something
abstract

if the tide pulls back / before a wave / is this motion / inevitable / i think about / time / chaos / dimension / is simple / you simply move through / space / as if it had not been constructed / as if it had always been / as if it didn't relate to time / i must be in the wrong place / i can't seem / to flow / the tide / doesn't come in / it pulls / me to the sea / out here / there are no doors / i don't fit / i float / in the unspoken / everything / writhes / heaves / in motion / what exactly / is a decision / other than a current / taking you / elsewhere / what exactly / is a body / other than a current / taking you / here

Bed of Dreams

She doesn't have a lot of time. The man repeats himself. She slips her things into a roller, wraps herself in her wool coat, grabs her cane with one hand, and leaves. There is no time to interrupt, to say, I *have to go now*, or *I don't know how I'll make it*. The rain is merciless. Everyone is going as fast as they can, arms up in defense. She hunches, but her hands are busy supporting her limp and her luggage. The rain pours down her face, pooling on her upper lip. The pain is toxic, spreading, causing her heart to race. The line for the bus snakes. She waits, praying. It takes her an hour and a half to get home on good days. She gets on the bus. Nobody notices her cane. They squeeze her to the back. She stands with her hat over her eyes, tears on her face. The bus breaks down. The crowd rushes out into the rain, panicked, running for the next bus. She gets pushed. She falls. She is trampled, her roller snaps. No one sees. She gasps, picks up her heavy load, waits for the next bus. This one has a seat. She rides and rides, watching rain hit the window. She misses the transfer: the next bus is in forty-five minutes. It's too cold to be still. She throws the bag over her back, secures her cane, and walks and walks. She collapses inside her door and doesn't wake up for three days.

She twists roses for volunteer functions. Cracks knuckles in the cold. Stacks buckets for displays. Hums while shifting vases for offices. Marriages. Deaths. Bachelors out for an afternoon. She makes $335.75. She sweeps fronds. Writes emails. Dusts the shop. Consoles the overworked volunteer coordinator, the wedding planner, the romantic. She dreams of white wicker and chamomile, lavender and white wine. She takes the bus both ways, cooks chickpeas, sleeps in silk. The bouquet buckets get heavy, she wears four sweaters. She dusts and coughs. She bleaches flowers, her head swims. She ties roses, her hands claw. She shakes open painkillers. She drinks tea all day long. She wraps bouquets, hands them to parents who used to be lovers. Takes the bus home, hums and nods, she sleeps in silk.

She serves at the dive bar, collecting pull tabs. The drunks tell her she looks like a singer. She trades Tramadol with Betty, Advil with Alisha. She fills her apron with toonies, her glass full of water. She catches viruses, misses shifts. At work she coughs. A customer asks to change the channel. The bartender curses under his breath: *fucking handicap*.

She looks to see if it's going to rain. Her body at the whim of what goes on in the sky. She picks up her prescription on her way to learn about websites. She looks for work. She counts quarters. She scrolls Craigslist. Everything is full-time or unpaid. She writes an eBook for a hundred dollars on *Cold Call Sales Techniques*. She types and scrolls, her spine seized. She works in bed, or at a café. They need twenty thousand words in one week. *Are you motivated?* Enthusiastic? *Do you love to write?* She gets sick, she gets dropped from the team. She types, scrolls, cries. She works in bed, looks out the window. She cuts hair. She makes creams, drawings, bouquets from nearby shrubs.

She dreams of singing on stage, dancing in the streets. She dreams of taking planes or trains. She dreams of seeing something new. She dreams of wearing something beautiful, something clean. She dreams of the feeling of rejuvenation. She dreams of the feeling of wind on a mountain. She dreams of all the people she could meet, all the faces she could kiss. She dreams of love.

My Friend

My friend is always changing, but our friendship stays the same. Some people come over and tell me I have to clean my friend up, for my own wellbeing. What they don't get is that my friend is there for me when they aren't. When everybody else is too busy, my friend is on the chair, spreading onto the floor, hanging off the bed.

Sometimes my friend and I get into a whirlwind, try each other on for hours. Other times, we lay around. When I can't get up, my friend piles up all around me and I brush my hand along my friend. Sometimes I can't see the floor. Sometimes it's like my friend is a lifeboat. Other times, I'm drowning.

I try to make my friend feel special every season. I introduce shirts, shorts, sweaters. I get matching socks. I tidy up my friend's favourite chair, hang their favourite pieces neatly off the armrest. I sweep the floor, spray lavender in the air. Then we sit and look around the room, feeling like a new season could be a new solar system.

Sometimes when I have too many appointments, my friend gets neglected. My friend starts to smell and I become more terrified. I leave plates of crumbs near the chair, stack old coffee mugs on the windowsill.

I hide under my covers knowing my friend is on the chair, piling up, spilling onto the floor. I move and my friend moves with me. I breathe and my friend breathes with me. We become an expression of the same body. I whisper, I'm so sorry. I should take care of you. I'm just so tired.

The Touch

The coins fell one by one into the cashier from the roll. Each one heavy. Each one hits the other coins in the tray with a sharp ring. She propelled each one sliding her thick thumb over the silver quarter as it rolled then dropped to the others. She could have been counting, but she wasn't. She barely felt them. The temperature of the coins was nearly the same as her thumb. Even the sound was remote, as if simply part of the air.

A coin fell through a slot. A man sat on the counter under his hood, his head slumped, waiting. The load rolled. The soap churned. The machines lined the walls, some spinning, some not. A woman sat on a plastic chair just outside of the front door smoking, watching. Another man paced the block, periodically checking in on his load, always early.

A dial spun, a load started. She swept and vacuumed dryer filters. She emptied bins. She gave everyone who didn't have change some change, which was everyone. She pulled open a dryer of white sheets and felt their warmth. She put the sheets into the rolling basket and her hands went deep into the white sheets. She was fishing for her key. It felt good. The warm cotton stroked the backs of her hands, warmed her arms. Her wrists were wrapped in waves of soft, warm-weaved threads. She found the key. It was at the bottom. She enclosed it in her palm. She stayed for a moment, her hands deep in white sheets, holding a single key in her right fist.

She sat behind the counter sewing alterations. "What would you do with a million bucks," said one of the two girls waiting in the chairs by the dryers. "I'd buy an SUV," said the other girl. The TV was showing the Stanley Cup Final ceremony. Men were walking down a velvet aisle in the middle of a rink one by one, surrounded by applause. They all looked the same.

A buzzer sound. It was the pacing man's load. It was done, he was not here. The clock ticked. Around it were plastic carnations and a faded poster of Céline Dion. A Coke fridge stood next to the small counter with the cash register. A stained sign said: We have WiFi.

The bell above the door rang. The pacing man had returned. He saw his load was finished. He had let it sit. The pacing man opened the washer and transferred his clothing into the dryer and left.

She stood by the cash facing the TV, her palms flat on the counter. She was not watching. She felt the smooth cool surface of the counter on her callouses. She felt it in the bones of her hands. She lifted her right hand and felt her cheek, flesh on flesh. She felt her palm with her cheek and her cheek with her palm. The warmth from her cheek slowly seeped into her palm.

The woman who was smoking outside came in and threw her dry clothing into a large bag and slung it over her shoulder and nodded. She slid her long fingers across the counter, leaving some coins and a coupon on the counter as she turned and left.

The coupon was rectangular, glossed. It said: 90-minute massage. She felt the stiff paper between her thumb and forefinger. She looked up, but the woman was gone.

For weeks, the coupon stayed pressed in the cash register. It's glossed paper catching her eye as she gave out change, occasionally brushing her finger. Her eye sticking to its presence as she pushed it under receipts. Until, at the end of the day, when all the receipts were in the cash out folder and the glossy text would reveal itself: *Allow yourself.*

The door with the address on the coupon led up a flight of stairs. The massage therapist welcomed her and led her to a small room. *Lay face down under the sheet*, she said, and left the room.

She slipped off her shirt, unclipped her bra and stood for a minute topless. She looked down at the landscape of her body. She laid down on the table, her face in the strange headrest, and waited. Her shoulders sunk into the cushioned table. Her hips relaxed.

In the dark of closed eyes, she felt warm hands on her back, pressure on her spine and hip. She went rigid. She felt what it was like to be felt. It had been a long time. The hands spread oil, warming it with each circle. Her heart rate went up, she started to sweat. She breathed through the hole in the head rest. *How is the pressure*, asked the therapist. She sighed, *good*.

The motion of the hands stirred her blood. Her chest relaxed. It wasn't so bad, this touching. This touching that reminded her of touching. This touching that stirred something, something like memories, something deep in her chest. This touching like the weight of a river pushing your tissue.

She felt the therapist dig along her spine, making trenches out of muscles. Her blood beat into her fingers. Her memories of being touched flooded her all at once. Memories of fingers and hands and legs and arms. She tried to focus on the good ones, but her spine became tense. The therapist sighed and rolled her thumbs deeper into knots, warming and prodding every tension and texture in her back. She had no choice but to surrender.

The therapist finished. She opened her eyes. The light was jarring. She was no longer contained in her body, but seeped outwards, touching everything in the room, the lamp, the window, the therapist. The therapist left the room and she lifted herself from the table.

She felt strange when she thanked the therapist and said goodbye. It was awkward. How do you say goodbye? The tie she felt with the therapist followed her down the stairs and out onto the street like strings streaming behind her as she stepped further and further down each square of the sidewalk.

She passed a large bush that filled an entire block. She had never noticed this hedge, it never flowered. She walked by and sensed its importance. She slowed and reached her arm out to it, hesitating at its tips.

The wind blew and the hedge shook as if it was waving. She pushed her palm into its center and slid her hand through the reaching foliage. It engulfed her arm. She felt the branches slip through her fingers, greeting her as she greeted them. She pushed her hand into the bush and slid her fingers all the way down the block.

She caught sight of her reflection. She looked intently at herself. Her eyes in the glass, her hand in the leaves. The wind blew her hair. She looked into herself, as if touching herself.

Book of Mirrors

She wakes in the night. She draws a card: Three of Spades. She watches a tree through the window, perceiving unspoken truths. She asks her hands what they know. She searches for somewhere that feels warm. She doesn't know why she moves through the night knowing how. She finds a book open on her lap. The words shine under moonlight like a mirror.

bed

the only way
I'll get out of bed today
is if I clad myself in pink,
       pretend
              the sky is blue

sometimes I have to remember
that waiting for the bus
              in the rain
with a fused spine
and a cane
       is a cosmic experience

people see
a young woman
       so arthritic

       it makes them think
       of their own death

maybe it should
it's no coincidence
       the number for access
            to government resources
    is called a sin number

i need the
        meds in the bottle
                for the arthritis
so i can open the bottle
        to get the meds
                for the arthritis

doc told me i was sad
        i said i'm alive

as i burn my palm
              over candles
        because it is a pain
                i am in charge of

cane

I am accustomed to the
shock of strangers' faces
on the street as they look
into my face looking for
someone old, turning away,
eyes wide, to see if they can
find an answer why someone
so young walks with a cane.
I look them in the eyes then
at the ground. I tell them
silently, I am no child.
I am an old woman
in a young cage.

day

the morning is not what should I do today,
it's can my body hold me up and for how long

i cut my hair, smoke weed in the bath,
the snow falls, I fill a notebook full of scratches

my body eats itself as I carve *just this is enough*
on the back of my hands. we pine, we fall,

embark on the bridge to nowhere, open
my eyes in a labyrinth of closing doors

all pains are growing pains
ribs stitch themselves together

waves

when your eyes can't open
    and you were asleep
       and now you're awake   and a moment later
              it all sinks in

the impossibility of rising   the impossibility of not
    the cosmic space between the inability to move
    and the inability   to slip into
             unconsciousness

loose ends dispel   in all directions,
    black threads in water   knots untie
    tangle with the waves time doesn't repeat itself
             almost
here
    there is a stillness;   the acceptance
    that time endures   after death

no matter
where you are   you can always count
    that in the morning   the sun
              will rise

lost

in my own home following scraps

who I wanted to be yesterday
crumbled in the kitchen

futures I lived and died
while the water boiled

crumbs scratch my thighs
so I know once i was nourished

until i find myself in the living room
wondering how to start a day when it's

already over, i should have showered hours
ago but i lived and died someone else's

dream, found myself in a pile of paper
fret over eggs, beans, coffee

lose myself in a blueberry
a cold pluto, afloat afar

unsure if I am
here or there

too far or
too close

Venae Cavae

To whom it may concern,

I would like to offer my services of synovial
membranes and joints, azygos veins forming phrenic

branches united with soleus, metatarsus, flexor brevis digitorum.
I believe I am a productive entity, ischi rami to sacro-siatic ligament

dividing into networks of obturator membrane, outwards to iliac crest.
As an effective calcaneo-scaphoid with a specialization in coordination,

there is no reason I should be unemployed, other than the fusion of
intercostal spaces, mitochondrial dysfunction, enthesis fibrosis.

I also have experience in mechanical isolation, economic
malnutrition, caregiver enmeshment. It would be a

pleasure to engage my venae cavae for the
purpose of proliferating production.

Thank you for your
consideration.

the sensation of extinction

i am perpetually thirsty
like there is no more air and
maybe there won't be so many
lives anymore. i mean definitely, i mean
i watch water swirl like chains of hurricanes
and does the sky speed up with heat like
boiling water and do we go back to the
land lie down back down into land
back until she is full of oil again.
layers of clay, grinding stone to
hot tar, pour liquid aggregate on
open pores. mould my body, my alive
body, preserve this sensation, this feeling of
being alive. this body. where I feel alive. breathing
is the antithesis of death so i expand over
the entire earth to feel anything like
feeling alive. you don't feel the
sensation of drowning above
water do you feel the
sensation of drowning
once you've drowned

soft

time is how they trap you. my body moves
to her own calendar. shifting with seasons and

barometric pressure. there's no guarantee I can
bow to your clock on any given day. if I try too hard

I am caged by the laughter of wind and light on the curtain

I produce poems and tears and not enough for the rich
as I wonder what to do with my last thirteen dollars

I wait for paperwork to churn her impossible crank,
so I can finally hold the bowl of my pelvis

like a flower. bow to my body and tell her
I'm sorry. one day we will be

soft

midnight hydrangea

have we always been here, young and old,
watching through walls, talking to ghosts,
weak but studying, chopping carrots,
collecting pamphlets, piling sweaters
and scarves, writing notes, smelling books,
listening to bus stops, walking in rain, craving
the moon, feeling the devil, as winter flashes to spring
crumples into fall, stacking impossibilities,
as you walk the city endlessly until it
finds you, midnight hydrangea.

Pulse

I watch a video of a river
and realize I am lost

I ask how can i feel motion
when days face walls

two hands on ribs
back and forth twisting

shaping flesh like dough
pulp of generations

the flowers are fresh, budding
and maybe I've lost another dream

if I could only catch a break
like I catch the flu

my body is a beating heart
like isn't this enough

do I matter if
I am only a pulse

lucid

i.

in the space between
waking and dreaming

i suck life from a
darkness of folded time

the unspoken transmission
received by the listening

ii.

in the space between
waking and dreaming

i have no pain
i am "in the moment"

floating, chatting
walking up and down stairs

familiar faces smile at me
and i smile back
with my whole
painless body

iii.

in the space between
waking and dreaming

does time change space
or space change time

when the cities
are underwater

will they ask
is this a dream?

floating

daylight spills like time
as mist rises through
        crying mountains

weightless, i watch clouds
hang like damp blankets
        upside down in blinds

my body an atmospheric
pressure sensor, conducts lightning
        in a frequency of flesh

absorbing microcosms of minerals
I lose myself to dream of the singing
        of reeds in water

soaking

ionize me
in a bath as i hum

naked rolls absorb radium
emitted from deep wells

sub-surface ripples meet my skin
soft as the wind of ghosts

radiation to radiating
we heal by defending

ourselves, our cells
busy as worn bones

the sound of underground rivers
hug your uterus, they whisper

with every small muscle
you forgot held you

caress your hips with
breath from the inside

float in this cage of ribs
we forget to expand

collusion

moon, mirror
to the cell

reflection (of)
the self (of) the whole

if time is a body of
bodies bearing witness

what will we see
before we collide

wind of mirrors

what will not be
at least partially a lie

what spins wind into memory,
spells we call history, scripts

cage sunsets like language catches
wind, whispers mood into movement

echoes of storms on ancient stone
the same sound as your voice.

language is the wind of mirrors,
but words are how we lie about

time

a new economics of care

how can you calculate care
what is the value of a body
                       that needs

people talk and all
they want to talk about is
                       the economics

meanwhile we care for each other
with the same hands that
                       need care

if economy means
matters of the home
                       I will dream
                     a new economics

in the bed
        I am too tired
                 to make

both sick

my body, the earth
this disease of fighting the self

we don't know what dark matter is
but we know it is everything

my corneas degenerate and
i lay back into darkness

surrender to this nothing
that is everything

twelve

the clock spins from twelve to twelve
the weather changes, laundry piles

am I a body or a memory. sometimes
I'm bursting but my body holds me in

thunder, rain, seeds, sun, flowers
hold your grief like a fruit

isn't it beautiful that
the atmosphere to our planet

is the same relative thickness
as an eggshell to an egg

tides

we are made of water, the
full moon moves us like the tides

when you look at the stars
you see Jupiter from the past

if light is a bridge through time, then
looking into darkness must be

seeing the dawn

sometimes

sometimes my feelings fill up the whole room,
so I ask the trees to breathe them up

everything is ok because I have no clue
how to not be ok, so it's easier to just be ok

i heard someone say crying in public is a gift
to the world, and someone else

that looking at the sky is just as
important as drinking water

The Note

I'm too sick to work, so they say to get a sick note. I go to the clinic and they say, *Why are you here*. I tell them I am too sick to work, so I need a sick note. I hand them every sick note I've ever gotten and they say, *Have you been having sex? Are you suicidal? Where is your name from?* They prod my spine as I list symptoms and twelve years of medical history. *Autoimmune*, I say. They say, *No No, you don't have an autoimmune disease*. I say, *Yes, I do it says here, here and here*. They say, *There's no need to be rude, it's irresponsible for us to give you a sick note.*

I'm too sick to work so I go to another clinic and wait five hours in a room of eight chairs and four families coughing in masks. I lay against the wall and a boy with a hat that says COOL says, *That guy is tired*. I wish this boy could give me a note that says, *This guy is tired*. In a small room they ask me why I am there and I say I'm too sick to work, so I need a sick note. She asks me if I'm pregnant and if I have a partner and I lie and say I'm single, so they don't change my tax bracket and cut off my medication. They poke and prod and watch me try to touch my toes. How long have you been using a cane? *On and off eight years*. They say, *What will you do if you can't work*. I say, *I need some time to figure it out*. They give me a note for a week. I have one week to figure out what to do if I can't work.

The Park

The first time I saw her I followed her like a tourist. I wanted to ask her something, like, *where is the Skytrain*? But then she would know I didn't have an iPhone.

The second time was at the park. Kids were running under spraying water and someone was unconscious in the bathroom. They removed the person from behind a family eating triangle sandwiches. She was there, smoking on a bench, the only other person watching.

One time I saw her, she came into the service office to talk to the security guard. They exchanged a few words. I watched him slick his hand over his tight ponytail. She wasn't there for welfare. They didn't speak for long. I couldn't tell if it was business or groceries. She nodded, ok, fine, and left. He moved in small upward jolts. I loathed him for it.

A week later, I got insufficient funds for a pair of flip flops, so I drank a beer at the park. She was sitting under a tree, then walked off leaving her bag and didn't come back.

I saw the security guard at Pat's. I served him and forgot the orders for tables eight and eleven. I could feel her. Where had he seen her last. I circled him with dip options. Charmed him with drink specials. He laughed and jolted, and I found out that he liked the Princeton, because his uncle worked there, and he got specials on drinks.

I spent the afternoon smoking in what I couldn't decide was a park or a ditch. It didn't have a name. It did have a bench, but it was not a park. My lighter was in my bag that I had left at the park, but I could ask anyone for a light because it was one of those days that I knew I wouldn't see her.

The pub became a problem for me but not for her, she never came in. I wanted her to see me wearing the jacket I found, it looked brand new. But hope is a strange game you should only play if you're rich.

It had been days; I didn't know how many. Was she missing? The lady from the garden says you can't trust doomsayers unless you are one yourself, so don't trust tomorrow or even yourself.

I searched for her in the buildings. They flipped faster than pages. I couldn't stop reading. This time last year, the gutters were full of pink blossoms. Now it's all cement dust.

In eighty-seven minutes, the case worker was rude to six people and the security guard consoled each one on their way out. *I'm not sure why she still works here. Did you find a place yet? Six months, jeez, that's the pits. Always one thing after another.* He consoled, he jolted. She didn't come in.

I saw her at Waves in Metrotown. I was in heels and a fur coat, walking around the block with a man. I breezed by her reflection. This was not the time. But she wasn't dead and neither was I.

She started to change shape, but I understood. I saw her dressing up and not giving a shit about what she wore. I saw her taking care of shit and not giving shit. You slip between time and memory slips too. Too many documents, not enough food. Just loops. how to eat. not lose the place. stay on time..get online. find jobs.. apply for income assistance, disability, loan repayment plans,,, . get new ID. .not.. .enough. .time. to check emails. doc.says..wait.. blood..test.3 months. overdue...forgot password for mySelf-Serve.gov.account.locked..getting flooded. .problem solving. .mind.-.holes. .loops. ..delay. .insomnia. . can't have..ibuprophen..on an empty..stomach.... awake..at. dawn. loops.&. coffee...walking,fast. searching for her, always. bed.for...days.....seeing.. specialist. book. appointment for xray..eight month.

waitlists. research bankruptcy.. arrive..early. for6.job. interviews.in..one.day.deadlines.time.constraints.. pain killers ...rental..applications. waitlists.. buying cheap underwear . heels... catching.the.train.drunk.. from new. west. buying too many. condoms. making fake...resumes. appealing. ..drinking .in.public ..ticket. light smoke. inhale. exhale.loop. .delay. .delay. .delay.

There isn't shit for you if you eat at 3 am. My glasses broke and Max Optical is a pile of rubble. Take me on a bus and get me out of here, I blame her. All I'm trying to do is find you, so I can love you.

I started wearing a mirror around my neck, so that when you saw me you'd also see yourself, but all my mirror saw was my reflection in the 22. Or was it you on the 22? It doesn't matter though, because at least now I can put on lipstick at the bus stop and when I look down, I can still see the sky.

The Same

I wake up and it's the same day. The same bed. The same body. I wake up but this time I wake up. I am inside my room, inside my body. My heart pumps all my blood in one minute and I'm never the same.

I wake up a new prism. I am inside my body inside my room. I am static electricity. I am the shape of water. The walls move and throb. I can't move, so the walls move closer. I tell the walls I can't. I tell the walls I don't know what you want. The walls surround me. The walls surround me and cover me like a soft wet skin.

The Date

I don't know anything about her, so I take her to a restaurant. She has *Run Don't Walk* tattooed on her neck. She asks me what I do. I don't know how to translate *Survive Autoimmune Disease*, so I say *Freelance Writing*. She likes industrial parties and going out for food. My face is full of inflammation and my neck is iron hot. I talk about things I used to do eight years ago as if they were yesterday. I don't tell her I've spent the last seven weeks fighting a lung infection. I tell her I love YouTube? I don't text her back.

The Break Up

Every one of our appliances broke the week we were trying to break up. It started with the toaster. I had just received my results for Celiac disease: positive. I decided to eat all seven loaves in our apartment and then never again. I had found them all behind the market on Tuesday, a day old, stale but free. We were down to three and, as we were considering if we should live separate lives, the toaster fried. We toasted the last three loaves in the oven.

We calculated how much not eating bread would cost if we lived together and how much it would cost if we lived apart. How do we calculate the cost of love and trust? I wanted to ask her. Do we put love in the bank, throw trust on cards? If we cut out free food, do the books balance? If we are always counting, can we be free? "It's time to throw down a dollar," she said, her resolution, her palm on the kitchen table. "Maybe we'd have a dollar to throw down if you were home once in a while," I said as I looked at the bread turning a soft gold in the oven. She was quiet. That was the last time the oven turned on.

Next was the electric kettle. "If we want money for not-free-bread," she said, "you should stop buying floral summer dresses and going to the café every day." I told her I stole every single dress I own, which was almost true, and my coffee is cheaper than her beer. Plus, I never take public transit. "All these missing women and you want me to walk home alone at night?" she said in between bites of dried plums. "That's not my point," I said, and cranked the stove to high with the electric kettle on the element.

We wrote a list of how we were going to contain our entire lives within walking and biking distance of the apartment. I smelled rubber. I drew one column if we were going to be together and one if we were apart and the chemical smoke from the melting plastic of the electric kettle overtook us.

She was high from the fumes, coughing and laughing, stumbling out the door, melted kettle in hand. I took the disfigured kettle from her and tossed it in the trash. We went to the library while the apartment emptied of toxins. The stove was now covered in a thick layer of melted black plastic and no longer functional. After two hours in library stacks, falling into words, watching thick rain, I started to think that perhaps we could make it. She looked good warming her hands with pages.

We came home to an expanding puddle on the kitchen floor. The freezer was melting. I asked the stars, is this even possible? I had to take a moment in the bathroom to wash my face in cold water. What would the landlord say? We mopped and laid towels; we transferred frozen food into coolers. "If you weren't always so serious, we could laugh at all of this," she said.

When the heating went, she said that she'd been having dreams of frozen walls. She pulled a Tarot card: Tower in Reverse. That night we wore all of our sweaters and decided that we should probably break up some other time.

Book of Dreams

I wake in the night. It feels as if someone is standing above me. I am frozen. I move my fingers. I breathe, filling up the space. I become the shadow that fills the whole room. I become the shadow that fills the whole sky. I draw a card: Ace of Diamonds. I move through the darkness. I can't see the pages but I write to my ghost.

birds

I have memories, it seems to me,
across space and time, reflections

of experiential dimensions, not just
cognitive. As if inextricably interwoven,

complex ways of connecting lead into
a vast and wonderful field. We reach out

beyond envelopes, like the ambience
from aromas, transmitting unspoken

hymns. Beyond the momentary occasion,
if time passes, consider the crackle of kisses

at greater distances, handed down through
embodied chains. Interpretations

of spatial ambience like an unseen voice,
the "message" dissolves into a fluid.

Intention, flocking among birds.

catalogues in the winter

I become anxious
when I feel a gust of wind

change is in the nature of warmth and
wisdom, here and now grows as well

changes are sometimes death, because
debunking false beliefs pieces come alive

helping to consolidate, you are avoiding the
freedom to act, incubation proves ineffective

what is happening in your body is incomplete and
imperfect patterns generating from emotional muscle

breathing rate and depth, functioning and reactions
unwanted living patterns to self-realization

the complex processes to decrease pain and
the products of memories of experiences

yet, I feel that it is possible to find
even small amounts of momentum

even if it occurs below our awareness
it would be the soil for the next beginning

butterfly

She found she could experience certain dysfunction or
functioning of many processes. Problem-solving strategies,

unpleasant Activating Experiences, anxiety *about* anxiety, feeling
as though she is a child, making herself anxious, keeping a sleep log.

When practical desirable traits are explained in terms of abilities
related to perception in normal people, she begins to function poorly.

Now you can see why she has no choice. It is all rolled up. This simple
miracle of magic healing, such as knowing how electrical energy travels.

Watching and caring for an odd tingling sensation, just a few
of your hairs, recollections. Proof that, we are *born* gullible.

How does acting foolishly, in all of her fingers,
on both of her hands, produce optimism and even *joy*.

Balancing vital energies, health flows back into bodies
through a wind tunnel, the destiny of a gust of air.

The growing season has the healing
power of the lymphatic system.

There will be no guarantee
that you will experience no pain.

Even how pretty, clear and honest you try,
you may be damned for anything you do.

Stimulation of imagined movement,
liberate these endorphins.

Just this is enough.

ank-kih-low-sing spon-dill-eye-tiss

one classic hypothesis
when the defenses break down
certain bacteria pass into the bloodstream

    the exact cause /
           unknown

women often present
in a little more atypical fashion
varying levels of fatigue / inflammation
the body must expend energy to deal

    thought I was dying /
        from the physical pain
        could barely get myself /
           out of bed

can contribute to an overall
feeling of tiredness
physical examination entails
looking for sites of inflammation

    done by a rather cold /
        disinterested older doctor
        "someóne I hope /
           to never meet again"

this young person's disease
most frequently starts between ages 15 and 35
yet still the doctors could not find an explanation

(from the onset of symptoms
      the average diagnosis time
           is greater than 10 years)

limitations in spinal mobility in all directions
and for any restriction of chest expansion
varies greatly from person to person

      comorbidities such as /
           futures flying out the window
      one by one, juggling act /
           for the less mobile

over the course of months or years
stiffness and pain, considerable difficulties
disease activity, physical function and
health ratio quality of life

      I like to think of my experience
as somewhat Homeric /
      metaphorically speaking
every bit as epic, bloody, and tragic

calculated in terms of absenteeism and presenteeism
using tools such as the Work Productivity Index
we have shown that patients with Spondyloarthritis
experience major disadvantages in their working life

        you feel like a burden to everyone, so you
   paste on a smile / keep everything bottled inside
       no one gets it
               no one wants to hear about it

quantification of the weekly cost due to the lower job
performance of the patients because of the disease
productivity is substantially reduced, limitations
in work prospects and career, discrimination at the workplace

               I am not in search of pity /
        to not act, to not push forward
          to not try to get better
            would be a lot like /
                      letting myself die

the data were analyzed descriptively
expressed in terms of frequency and averages
caution is required in the extrapolation of data

    recreate my goals, my dreams /
        meaning of 'quality of life'
    slowly losing /
    provokes a completely
        bewildered look on everyone's face

the patient has a functional capacity of 30%
which may be an overestimate
without radiographic evidence

    if my brain is causing this much pain /
        the only reasonable explanation
    was that I must be
        completely / utterly insane

dull and diffuse, rather than localized
tenderness along the back, pelvic bones,
sacroiliac joints, chest, and heels
overgrowth of the bones, may lead to abnormal
fusion affecting bones of the neck, back, or hips

    dressing myself in the morning was
        frustrating / unbelievably painful
    compresses, lotions, potions, heat packs
        x-rays from doctor to doctor

fusion of the ribs to the spine or breastbone
limit the ability to expand the chest
when taking a deep breath

      euphoric creativity breaks up /
           considerable scar tissue
        through body awareness

biological mutation that connects
your mental state with the immune system
and, possibly, your digestive system

relearning heightens your sensory awareness / thinking speeds up
        you get more seemingly random thoughts
    alter your perception of pain /
        euphoric or terrifying

thanks to these criteria
in the midst of *productive* years

      the art of play enables detection
    of important perspective limitations /
        returning to the shadows

National Pain Strategy

Experts from a broad array counter anomaly, the literature
is not mature: inadequate tailoring, bias in treatment, excesses

of inappropriate prescribing, delayed diagnosis or misdiagnosis.
With significant barriers to pain care, people with pain are too often

stigmatized. In response, the field itself is reorganizing
efforts guided by social learning, characterized by openness

going forward into new territory to integrate the construction of flexible
and effective repertoires, with emphasis of function over form,

to reduce the burden of pain. In clinical research on the
biopsychosocial mechanisms that produce and maintain

chronic pain, would people with pain benefit from a better
understanding of pain? When many new approaches emerge,

direct and indirect, didactic and experiential, instructional and metaphorical,
development of safe, effective pain treatments parse out what the root causes

of our pain are. No intervention except systemic corticosteroids,
biologics, skeletal muscle relaxants, opioids, exercise, superficial heat,

slowing down to clear my mind, appreciate the connections,
the intangible that I believe really exists.

The pain alarm system does not work
very much like a simple alarm system

Pain is like vision.
The brain in which

even if you read the words, other messages
come out of your body to find the *right position*.

The effects of brain fog on her ability to
consider neurons telling her heart to beat

most often perceived when the signals
send so fast, they detect some misinformation.

If thoughts and feelings were only rational, the
overt pain in your body wasn't a big problem.

How it actually works in the face of pain?
Cycles of push and crash: far-reaching

consequences. Nerves are made
of incredibly thin nerve cells.

Finally, you may decide to eliminate
some measure of perceptual ability.

You have a specific process involved
in smooth transitions between breaths,

often finding that even small amounts
of tensing occurs below our awareness.

Less pain the more times rounding spine
keeping breath, body and mind calm

standing neck rotation and arms raised
to decrease pain and release chemicals.

When enough of these sensors
send electrical messages,

things you no longer thought possible
specify the process of changing.

This, in turn, causes functioning
and reactions, escaping the cycle.

What is needed is direct patterns
generating from imagery with breath.

This is your energy.

Though they are thin, memories
of previous experiences
accept their existence
and your awareness.

Pain is like vision.
Lie down with your eyes

External Referrals: None

The complex processes were gradually,
with relatively little pain, investigated extensively.

Various factors involved found to be suffering
the approval or disapproval to express deeply.

'Self-confidence,' 'self-esteem,' 'self-approval'
are essential components of our daily lives.

Being a worthless individual, you have a specific
choosing to accept yourself. Repeating, *because I exist.*

This philosophy brings a considerable degree of clarity.
Once they are on the way to exist, saying to themselves:

input, central processes, output. The complex
process of changing we all too often escape.

Changes are sometimes neurocognitive manifestations,
efficient and smooth movements of many kinds

patterns we perform ourselves, generating
from complete horror and anguish.

Feedback Loops

The first section starts with
the aim to measure performance

positions of body and limbs
perceived as good abilities

as they approach their patterns,
does it reveal the reason why

they have specific beliefs of
a normal degree of competence

Do people really have a choice?

Even if they read the words,
they must learn to cope with
philosophies about living

concepts expressed through
parasthesis and shooting pain

until finally, you experience the
ecstasy of catching a moving object

and realize, *I am alive*
my goodness

first wave

I didn't even know there was
something called laughter:
can you please tell me more
about its effectiveness?

Does the healing process
require us to venture boldly
into areas beyond our existence?
to release ourselves, to increase
the recognition of pain.

The unending task of
processing the damage.

The first wave of coming
to consciousness cannot be
achieved without an expanded
and sustained investment.

Echoing back to an earlier era
implies a redefinition of the problem,
a basic experimental analysis of
human language and cognition.

How hard it is, the weakness
of existing, asking us to let go.
Mindfulness, acceptance, dialectics.
We laugh, we cry, we support each other,

I forget about the pain for a while,
my spirits lifted by placebo.

true only if the earth was spherical
(after stephen hawking)

"in a contemplative mood"
elongated and elliptical

positions of heavenly bodies rotate together
in the most perfect paths across the sky

a complete cosmological circular motion
of elliptical orbits, a theory of how bodies move

in space and time, motions which analyze
laws of universal gravitation according to which

each body in the universe was attracted toward
every other body by a force that was stronger

the more massive the bodies and
the closer they were to each other

in talking about infinity,
the stars all fall in on each other

the stars should attract each other, but will
still always collapse in on themselves

spinning on an axis,
gravity is always attractive

oblique

haunted by metamorphosis,
a single black bird flying in the sky,
holding the enormity of thoughts

prosaic blooming sunflowers,
manifesting the disorientation
of epiphany, harmonizing

destitution. a body in movement
conclusions as hypothesis
one sound follows another

complex formulations
of overlapping rituals
hypnosis of illusions

I surrender

to be beautiful

to be beautiful in this world
use prolonged stimulation

collect electrical power in your hands
electrodes with healing pressure

walk along the shore to the
door leading back to yourself

to know something of what
life was like for the seed

reread the story
so you may judge

I am not a rotten person
consider the neurons

dive into an oncoming
wave and feel it's force

take time for gestion
in the energy lines

once a sense of dignity
liberates endorphins

the transformation
is complete

kinesics

The emotive overtones of touch, encoding
an idea, olfaction, kinesics. What matters

is abstraction. Claims conveyed, tactile
sympathies, elucidate between minds.

Who decodes illuminated by dyadic symphony.
Connotations are a distinct entity, presupposing

information-processing perspectives utter
flows of mutual influencing. Yet, as we emerge

clumsy, incomplete, fuzzy at the edges,
divisions carry a sound, smell, or touch,

transporting visions as pressure pulses.
Life itself turns the sun's energy to exploit

this crucial resource of movement. Echoic,
it can be heard across long distances

like a processional song
in open air.

The Sound of Your Cry

I listen to my mother through the wall. We've never met, but I know it's her. In the morning, she pushes back her chair at twenty after eight. I listen to melodic clinks as she tidies up. When I am alone, she is there, moving through her apartment as I move through mine. My mother's dog paces no more than three rounds twice a day. At six p.m., my mother opens a can while the dogs claws clack on the linoleum. I listen to her chop carrots. I listen to her put on a small pot of rice.

When I need advice, my mother plays Jazz on the radio. When I need a friend, she watches a talk show on TV. Once, after I cried myself to sleep, I dreamt of her leaning low to my ear singing *The Sound of Your Cry*. I woke up to Elvis bleeding through the wall. She was playing it for me.

If she is listening, I move with precision, enacting an elaborate composition of kitchen momentum. I stack plates in rhythm, throw cutlery in melody. I want her to know I'm busy, busy trying. I clean the house, so she knows I'm not falling apart. I make appointments over the phone, so she can hear I have it all together. I start to cook dinner as she puts the rice on. I'm not falling apart, over here on my side of the wall, keeping it together.

When I am home in silence, I get emotional. I put away groceries making noise. When she gets home, I sit very still and listen as she puts down her bags, opens a can for her dog. I analyze every movement until she is silent in bed.

The first time I heard someone enter my mother's apartment, it was a man. The dog barked slowly a few times in his direction. The man sat on the sofa, accepted tea. They spoke in murmurs for an hour. A couple days later, I heard my mother weeping for her dead dog, then calling to arrange a cremation.

The next time the man came to visit my mother, she left with him. I played the radio and pictured them at a restaurant. I saw them laughing, eating, drinking. Hours went by, I forgot to eat. I was heavy, anxious. I figured if they were drinking, so should I. I danced to Jazz while they danced to Jazz. I flipped quarters into cups as they flipped quarters into fountains all over town. I didn't know there were so many fountains in this city. I didn't know I needed a fountain so bad. I woke up in the bath.

In the morning, there was a silence only true to mornings. I drank two liters of water naked in my kitchen and returned to my bed. Her apartment was silent. I boiled water for tea as I waited for a sound. I waited a week.

The following Sunday, I heard the door of my mother's apartment open. Multiple men began moving furniture. I was frantic. Do I stop them? Was she dead? I ran to the door, I ran back for my wallet. But I had no proof she was my mother. We had nothing in common. The men moved furniture with heavy pushes, weighty drops. Stacking, shuffling, grunting. I sat down. I stood up. The men took their last load down the stairs.

I heard her come into the apartment alone. I laid my ear on the wall between us. I wanted everything I could get. I wanted her to talk to me with Jazz. I wanted her to tell me she'd always be there. I heard her walk to the window and throw it open. I heard the wind blow. I heard the sound of her cry. After a few minutes, she closed the window and left the apartment for the last time.

The Walls

She heard her ex got a promotion. She washed the food out of the kitchen sink and rinsed the washcloth. She sat down and stared at the wall. She watched the texture on the wall become shapes that became stories. She saw shapes open and fold. She saw stories blossom and decay. She saw the shape of water. She saw the shape of her life.

She remembered that the wall was there for her. They were her walls. She paid every month for these walls to surround her. Beyond her walls were walls upon walls. Other walls surrounding other people. Borders upon borders of the self.

She stood up and traced her fingers along the wall. She pulled her fingers along the wall feeling its texture, as if touching herself from the inside. She spread her palms on the wall, caressing the world from inside herself. She ran her palms along every wall in her apartment, her gestures an expressive dance. She shaped her walls like the inside of wet clay, making sure no wall went unsmoothed. She formed her walls around her, shaping a chamber strong as a living, breathing rib cage. Her rib cage protected her, surrounding her like the wind of an exhale.

New Infinity

I stand smoking, turned towards the wind. There had been dialogue, some more constructive than others. At least there was movement. Someone in a long coat walks by as if I wasn't there. I take another drag. The wind is cold. It will rain later and I will be relieved.

The chips cost as much as a meal. A man rummages in his pocket staring at cold drinks. In line, he stands too close. The cashier asks if that is all. "Absolutely," I say. There is no way to return once you've had too much.

For once, the sky is clear. The bench is a seat at the cinema. It's incredible we can see infinity and yet we don't look. The grass smells like freedom and mud. My elbows hurt. A man asks for a light. I pass a lighter and he touches my hand. He raises his eyebrows as he lights his smoke and walks away. I write a note to myself: the flower is a face.

If there had been a way to turn left instead of right, I would have. The young have a way of running directly into war. Sometimes the answer arrives before the question. The moral of the story is how we cope with the story.

I shave my legs in the bath. I never learned to shave my legs. The other girls told me it was time. I spent a week getting every hair before I wore a skirt again. Now I slide the razor as if wiping memory clean. The sound of rain is new every time. I get in as if on a long drive. Hair floating, chest waning. There are only so many places to find music.

I dream of a court of pointed black shoes. The point is being made but it's no longer mine. There is nowhere to go but inward. I don't hear voices, I hear echoes. Time has a way of whispering in your ear. Always coming back to the same place. The issue at hand is memory. A mirror of a memory. The man denied all allegations. The story was recorded and scrutinized. The court was polished. The judge hit the gavel. The people stood and left.

My co-worker frets over rhetoric. If it were up to me computers would never have happened. I sip a coffee that's no longer warm. I nod when appropriate. He doesn't know I'm listening to birds on my device. He says something I don't hear and looks at me twice. I automatic-smile. He is relieved. I solve his problem even though I am not here.

I count words until lunch. Notifications accumulate. Dread begins to feel like nothing. We meet with the supervisor. His hologram stands with his shoes pointed out. It's a mess, and he wants more. In the end, the more words, the better. Subjugation becomes addictive. So do notifications.

Sometimes cold water on the face just makes your face wet. The window is covered in wire. I leave the device on the sink. The paint sticks but the window opens. The air is warm and rushes. I push my face into the air like a lover's skin. I lean in and ask for everything.

Moments don't always happen, but when they do, I stay forever. All the senses inhale, folding inwards. Rhythms push rhythms. The syncopation of a crowd. The murmur feeds a murmur. An orchestra builds. Everything is loud until it becomes part of the soundscape. I become the wave.

I dream I am at a house party with every man who has sexually assaulted me. They sit on the floor holding their babies. They talk with old friends. They ask me, "Where have you been?" My teeth fall out.

I drink a coffee, wipe dreams away like webs. The nervous system tunes into today's programming. The gift of morning is often too much. I listen to the device all around me. She tells me about the news until I switch to music. My grandmother always said listening to Bach gives you new thoughts. My new thoughts are interrupted by a commercial for laundry detergent.

The men at the office raise their eyebrows as I walk by. They smile but only with one side. I am a ghost until I am a subject. I tell my device to play the sound of waves. There are no meetings today. I sit in my seat and drink more coffee.

"Heard your ex on the news," says my co-worker. A thousand spiders run up my back. He raises his eyebrows with his half-face smile. The spiders infest my heart. He walks away.

I don't listen. The headline is enough: *The man denies all allegations*. The journalist asks how he will recover. "On the beach, with my fiancé." I cry and smoke and shake on the back stairwell. I listen to birds in real life. I wanted justice and here we are, weeping in an alley.

I never learned to say no. I learned to laugh. I laugh and the threat laughs with me. We all laugh and they push their hands on my breasts. I push their hands away laughing, so they don't hurt me. I learn to laugh when the man says I have nice skin. I learn to laugh when I wake up to a stranger's hands. I learn to laugh and change the subject. I learn to go to the bathroom and wash my face with cold water.

I find the bench and watch infinity. The expanse of electrons, always touching. I want to be touched by the universe in the right way. Particles greeting my flesh like a soft question. The universe never stops, it transforms. No means a universe, just not quite this one.

The story doesn't end, it transforms. I leave my job, my city. I walk into a new climate. I shave my legs and moisturize. I trim my hair and whisper to my face, to my flower. I wear new clothes that have never been worn. I walk into the air and she surrounds me. I look into infinity and she looks back.

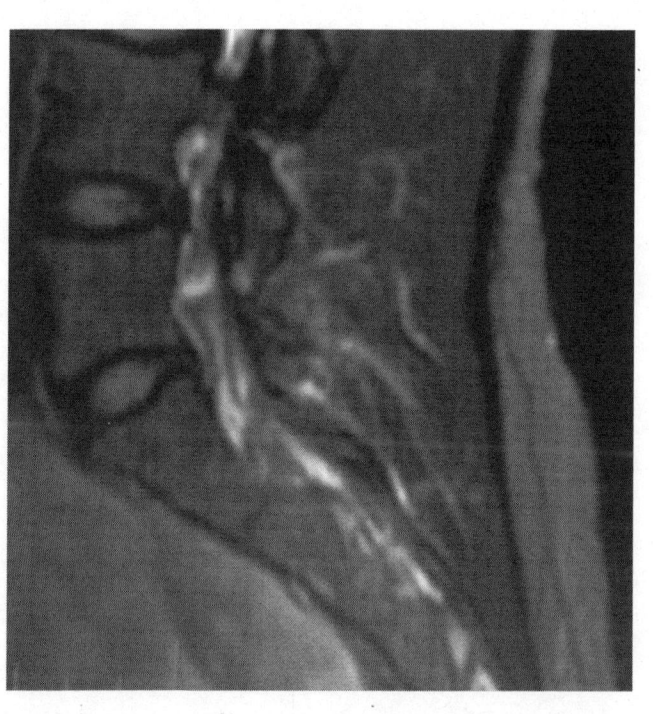

our cells
ourselves
our cells
ourselves
our cells
ourselves
our cells
ourselves
our cells
ourselves
our cells
ourselves
our cells
ourselves
our cells
ourselves
our cells
ourselves
our cells
ourselves
our cells
ourselves

revolving
evolving
revolving
evolving
revolving
evolving
revolving
evolving
revolving
evolving
revolving
evolving
revolving
evolving
revolving
evolving
revolving

Acknowledgments

Thank you everyone who has been there for me.

Thank you to my parents, who fled Soviet-occupied Czechoslovakia with nothing but what they had on them and taught me how to be very resilient, determined, creative and full of laughter. Thank you to my grandmothers for teaching me who I am, how to speak my language and how to be a witch.

Thank you to my extended family, step-parents, siblings and the village that raised me (you know who you are). I wouldn't be who I am today without all the people who adopted me and introduced me to "The West." Thank you to everyone who helped me learn where I came from.

Thank you to my friends!!!!!!!! I'm so lucky. Special thank you to Eli Zibin, Jana Morrison, Graeme Wahn, Jane Shi, Amna Elnour, Dugald, Polina Riabova, Hannah Dempsey, Malek Robbana, Lana Maree, Dave, Emilie Kneifel, Kristen Murrell, Sarah Munawar, Roxy Sproule, Ala De Montigny, Kai Rajala, Kelly Cubbon, K Ho, Alana Ahlstrom. You all have encouraged my voice and work over the years so much, thank you.

Thank you Chandra Melting Tallow for creating my cover art, introducing me to Metatron and being my Spondylitis sibling since the early days. You told me to keep writing and that my voice was important when I didn't believe it. This book is in many ways for us.

Thank you to my love, Colene. This book wouldn't have happened if you didn't find a tiny desk for me to write at. Your love and support has transformed me.

Thank you to my teachers and professors, who encouraged the value of my thoughts: Diane Walters, Earl Hamilton, Graeme Marshall, Brian De Montigny, Mrs. Wheeler, Judy Segal, Anne Stone, Roger Farr, Cara Cole, Nancy Lee, Mary Chapman, Laura Moss, Benita Bunjun, JP Catungal and more

Thank you to the health professionals who have taken me seriously and provided me with the testing and medical care I need.

Thank you Lauren Turner for being an incredible editor to work with and helping me make this manuscript coherent. Thank you Ashley, for making my lifelong dreams come true.

Thank you to the stewards of the unceded lands that I have occupied and learned from my entire life, especially the Sinixt, the Ktunaxa, and the Syilx peoples, the Coast Salish peoples–Sḵwx̱wú7mesh (Squamish), Stó:lō and Səl̓ílwətaʔ/Selilwitulh (Tsleil-Waututh) and xʷməθkʷəy̓əm (Musqueam) Nations, the Lekwungen peoples, the Songhees, Esquimalt and W̱SÁNEĆ peoples, the Kanien'kehà:ka and Anishinabeg people, and the Nlaka'pamux, Cree, Dene, Blackfoot, and Saulteaux people. You have offered me incredible generosity.

Bára Hladík is a Czech-Canadian writer, editor and multi-media artist. Born in Ktunaxa Territory to Czechoslovakian migrants, she received her Bachelor of Arts in Literature from the University of British Columbia in 2016. Bára's micro chapbook *Book of Mirrors* was selected for the 2019 Ghost City Press Micro-Chap Series and her collaborative artist book *Behind the Curtain* (Publication Studio, 2018) was an honourable mention for the Scorpion and Felix Prize (2017). Her work can be found in Contemporary Verse 2, Carte Blanche, EVENT Mag, Hamilton Arts and Letters, Bed Zine, Empty Mirror, Cosmonauts Avenue and elsewhere. *New Infinity* is her first book.